LITTLE BROWN BEAR
Has Fun at the Park

Written by Claude Lebrun

Illustrated by Danièle Bour

ℚℙ Children's Press®

A Division of Grolier Publishing

New York   London   Hong Kong   Sydney
Danbury, Connecticut

Mama Bear
brings Little Red Bear
and Little Brown Bear
to the park.
They want to go down
the big slide.

They climb to the top
of the slide.
Little Brown Bear
does not want to be
the first to go down.

Little Red Bear
goes first.
She likes the slide.
She tells
Little Brown Bear
it is fun.

Little Brown Bear
is afraid
to go down the slide
alone.
He starts
to climb down.

"Little Brown Bear,"
says Mama Bear.
"We will go down
the slide together."

Down the slide
they go!

Little Brown Bear
wants to go again.
He is not afraid
of the slide anymore.

This series was produced by Mijo Beccaria.

The illustrations were created by Danièle Bour.

The text was written by Claude Lebrun and
edited by Pomme d'Api.

English translation by Children's Press.

Library of Congress Cataloging–in–Publication Data

Lebrun, Claude.

Little Brown Bear has fun at the park / written by Claude Lebrun;
illustrated by Danièle Bour.

p. cm. — (Little Brown Bear books)

Summary: Little Brown Bear is afraid to go down the big slide
at the park, so he and Mama Bear go down the slide
together and then he is not afraid anymore.

ISBN 0-516-07846-1 (School & Library Edition)

ISBN 0-516-17846-6 (Trade Edition)

ISBN 0-516-17805-9 (Boxed Set)

[1. Bears — Fiction. 2. Fear — Fiction.] I. Bour, Danièle, ill.
II. Title. III. Series: Lebrun, Claude. Little Brown Bear books.

PZ7.L4698Lfge   1996

[E] — dc20   95-26329

CIP

AC

English translation ©1997 by Children's Press

A Division of Grolier Publishing Co., Inc., Sherman Turnpike, Danbury, Connecticut 06813

Originally published in French by Bayard.

Published simultaneously in Canada.

Printed in Belgium

1 2 3 4 5 6 7 8 9 00 R 06 05 04 03 02 01 00 99 98 97